For Will

Balzer + Bray is an imprint of HarperCollins Publishers.

Snail Crossing
Copyright © 2020 by Corey R. Tabor
All rights reserved. Printed in the United States of America.
No part of this book may be used or reproduced in any manner whatsoever without written
permission except in the case of brief quotations embodied in critical articles and reviews.
For information address HarperCollins Children's Books, a division of HarperCollins
Publishers, 195 Broadway, New York, NY 10007.
www.harpercollinschildrens.com

ISBN 978-0-06-287800-7

The artist used pencil, watercolor, colored pencil, and ink, assembled digitally,
to create the illustrations for this book.
Typography by Dana Fritts
20 21 22 23 24 PC 10 9 8 7 6 5 4 3 2
❖
First Edition

SNAIL CROSSING

Corey R. Tabor

Balzer + Bray
An Imprint of HarperCollinsPublishers

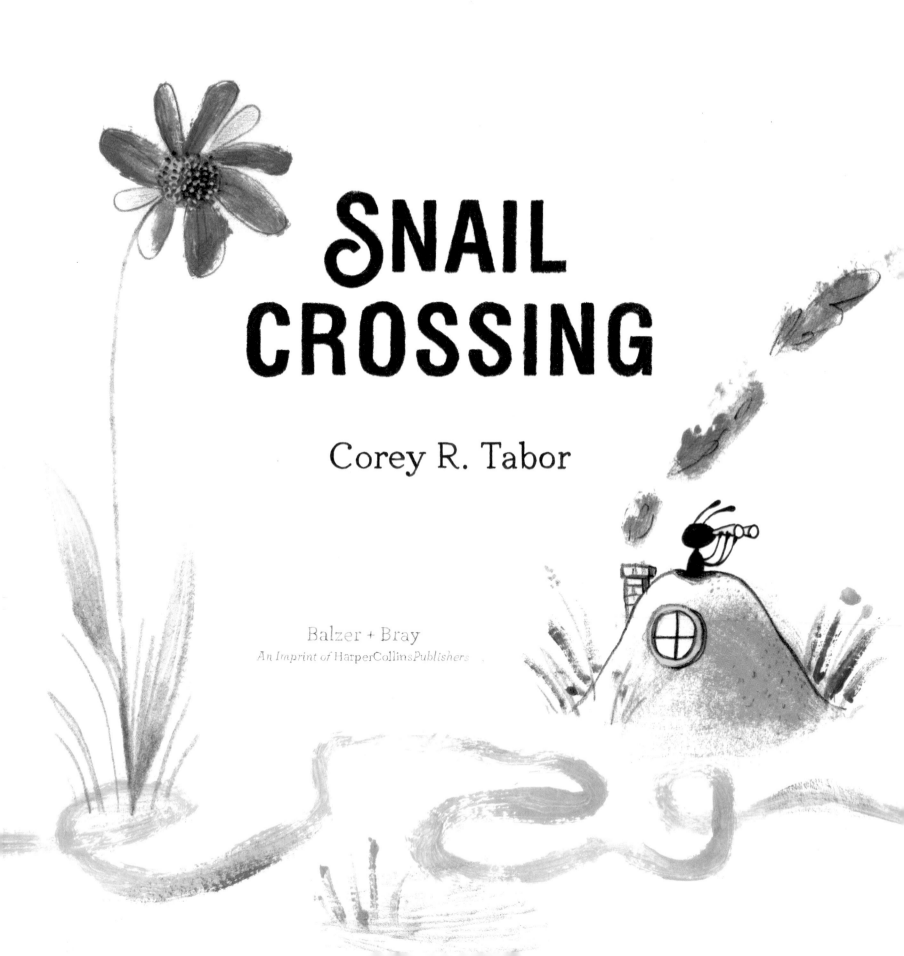

One lucky day Snail was out scooting around when he saw the most beautiful sight—

a field of plump, crisp cabbage just across the road.
"Well, you won't stop me!" said Snail to the road.

Snail had been traveling for some time
when he decided to take a break.
Why, I must be nearly there, thought Snail.

He was watching the grumbling gray clouds
when he felt something coming his way. What
it was, Snail couldn't say. Some things are too
big and fast for snails to ponder.

"Well, you won't stop me!" said Snail to the thing.
Snail was cabbage bound! Nothing could stand in
his way!

"Hey!"

"You!"

"You're standing in our way!"

"We've got a road to cross here!" yelled a troop of rowdy ants.

And they probably would have carried on like that if it hadn't started to rain.

"Rain!" cried the ants. "Help! Help! Help!"
Cabbage bound or not, Snail couldn't just
leave them there.

"Come in!" said Snail. "Come in before you drown!"

"Tea?" asked Snail.

"Oh!"

"Please."

"Thank you."

"That would be lovely,"
said the ants.

CLICK.

"We're sorry."

"About earlier."

"Terribly sorry."

"Sometimes we get a bit antsy,"
said the ants.

"Oh, I know the feeling," said Snail,
and he told them all about the plump,
crisp cabbage just across the road.

"Hmm," said the ants. *"Hmm."*

When the rain stopped, the ants said thank you, thank you, thank you, and goodbye.

"Well, I hope you'll come back soon!" said Snail.

"Count on it," said the ants, and off they went.

"Now, where was I?" said Snail to himself. "Ah, yes . . ."

Snail was cabbage bound!
Nothing could stand in his way!

Snail was scooting right along when he
noticed something standing in his way.
"Lunch!" said the hungry crow.

"Well, you won't eat me!" said Snail. "Can't you see I'm cabbage bound? Evasive maneuvers! Evasive maneuvers!"

HONK
HONK

And just like that, the hungry
crow was gone!

Snail was very relieved but a little dizzy from all that spinning.

Snail scooted

and scooted

and scooted

and . . .

"Hooray!" said Snail. "I made it!"

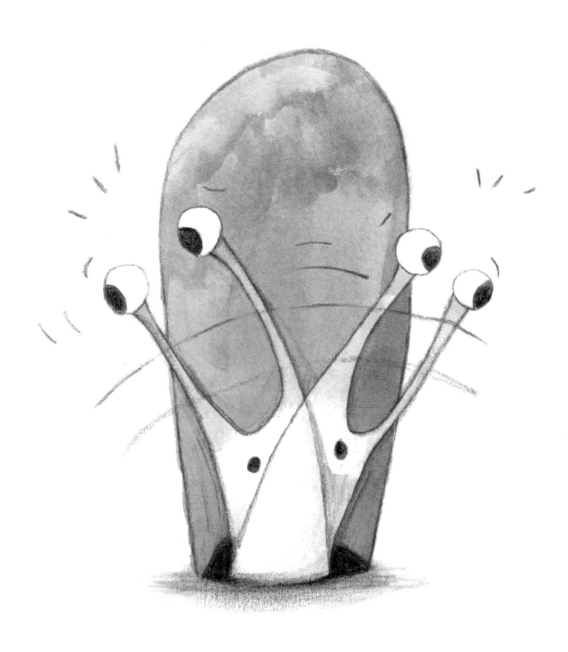

But where was the cabbage?

"Well, shoot," said Snail.

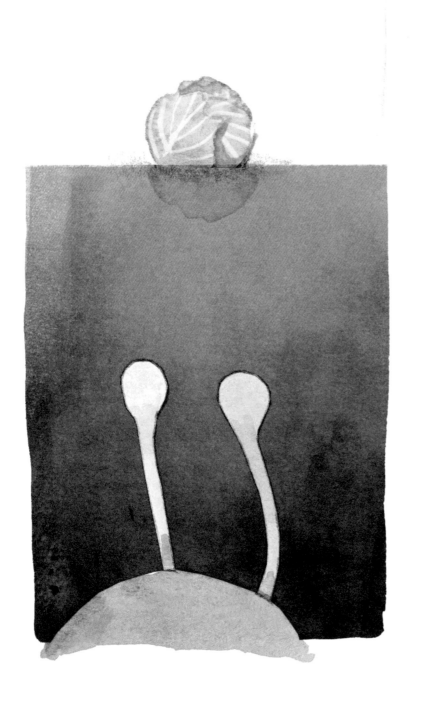

But what was that on the horizon?

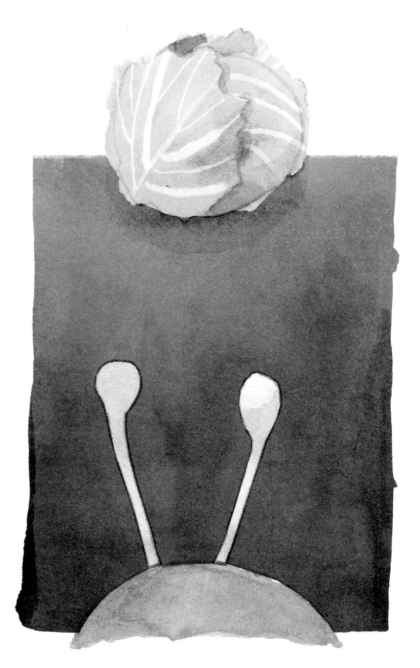

Could it be?

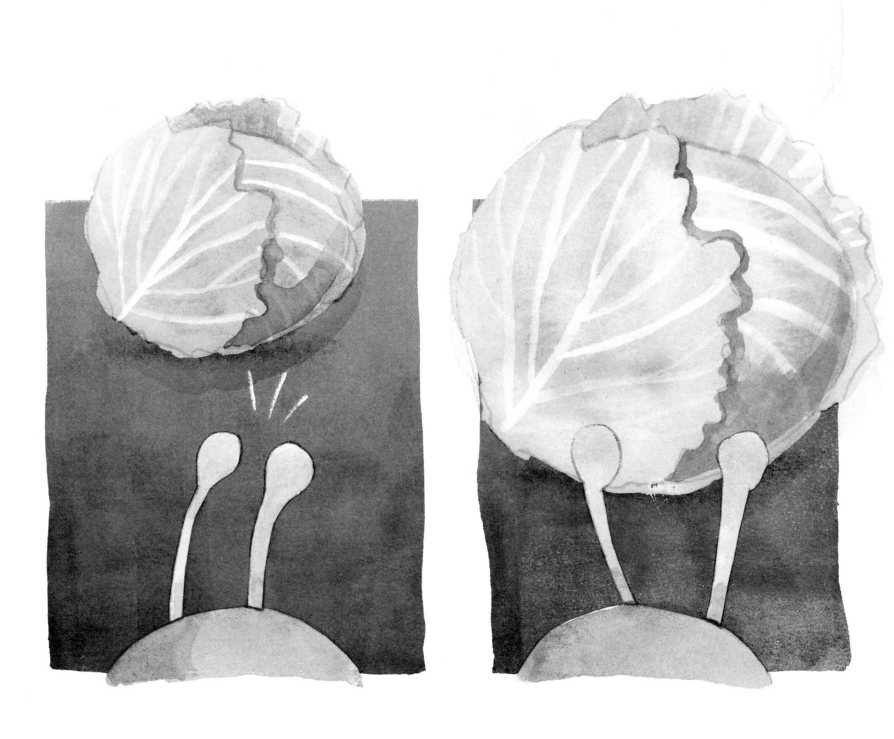

It was!   The cabbage was coming to Snail!

"Hooray!" said Snail.

"Thank you," he said to the ants. "Thank you, thank you, thank you."

Then the new friends went inside for cabbage soup and tea. And no one felt antsy at all.

the end